Copyright © 1990 by Nord-Süd Verlag AG, Gossau Zürich, Switzerland
First published in Switzerland under the title *Kleiner Vogel, flieg ganz hoch*
English translation copyright © 1990 by Naomi Lewis

First published in Great Britain, Canada, Australia
and New Zealand in 1990 by North-South Books, an imprint
of Nord-Süd Verlag AG, 8625 Gossau Zürich, Switzerland

British Library Cataloguing in Publication Data is available.

ISBN 1-55858-095-6

1  3  5  7  9  10  8  6  4  2

Printed in Belgium

Pirkko Vainio

# Fly High,
# Little Bird!

Retold by
Naomi Lewis

North-South Books

"I shall do it today," said Anton the fisherman. He was old, and for some time now he had not been strong enough to take his boat out to sea. He had made up his mind. He would sell the boat and live on the fruit and vegetables that he grew in his garden. He still had his tiny rowing boat; maybe he could catch a fish or two now and then in the river. It was nothing like the sea, of course.

His fishing boat was a good one and he sold it quickly. He sat for a while, looking at the scene he knew so well, then started off for home.

That afternoon Anton
went to work in his garden.
But his mind was still on
the boat which he had sold.
"Ah, the freedom of the sea," he said
to himself. "I shall never know that again."

He looked at an old wooden bird-cage which hung
on the wall. A sea captain friend had given it to him
long ago, with a bird inside; but Anton had straightway
opened the door and set it free. Now, trailing plants grew
over the cage, and sparrows used it to perch on while
they pecked at seeds. Those sparrows knew what
freedom was.

It was hard for Anton to keep away from the sea, and the very next morning he set out for the harbour. Perhaps he would see a few old friends there; he might even have a last look at his boat.

But when he reached the market-place he stopped, in horror. At one corner were rows of imprisoned birds in cages like the one in his garden. "Those birds—what are you doing with them?" he asked the man who seemed to own them. "Why, selling them, of course. What else would I be doing?" Poor Anton! He could not bear to see the caged birds any longer. He turned round and went home as quickly as he could.

He spent the rest of the day chopping wood. It suited his feelings. His shock had turned to anger; with each blow on the wood he became angrier still. "How can people cage up creatures meant to fly?" he asked himself. But he had no answer.

That night he had a strange dream.

In the dream his room was full of twittering birds. They flew around, beating their wings, until they had arranged themselves all around him as he lay in bed. Then they settled down, fixing their eyes upon him. They gazed and gazed—and he knew that the birds were asking him for help.

Then Anton awoke. It was very early dawn, but he dressed, went down to the river, stepped into his tiny boat, and began to row. As he pulled the oars, his ideas became clearer, and by the time he returned to the river bank he knew what he would do.

Anton took the money he had made from the sale of the boat and went down to the village. Even from a distance he could see the cages. He found the fat dealer and said to him firmly, "I'll have those birds." "Those?" said the dealer, pointing to the two nearest. Anton shook his head. "No, I want them all. Just tell me the price."

The birdseller saw that he had a good customer, and rubbed his hands with pleasure. He murmured some calculations, then named the amount. Anton gave it to him at once, and the two parted. They both felt cheerful, the birdseller because he had done good business, Anton for other reasons. He took as many cages as he could carry, and brought them to a field in the nearby open country.

Once there, he put down the cages, went back to the market-place, and fetched the next lot. At last, all the cages were in the field. By now the day was nearly over; twilight was falling. Anton felt very tired. The darkness made the birds rest too, in the cages, and Anton lay down among them. He fell asleep at once.

Shortly before sunrise the birds began to chirp softly. Anton woke and smiled. He picked up the first cage, lifted it high, spoke a few gentle words—then opened the door. "Fly high, little bird!" he called out. "No one will ever stop you flying again. You shall sing because you are free." He opened one cage after another.

Soon the air was filled with the sound of whirring wings. The birds flew hither and thither, sometimes high up in the air, then down again as if they could not be sure that they were really free. Whistling, trilling, piping, singing, they circled again and again round the old fisherman. And in the midst of all this, Anton danced on the grass and ran to and fro with outstretched arms, until he felt that he himself was flying.

At last the birds began to fly towards the horizon, further and further, until they could not be seen at all. Anton gazed after them for a long time. He had never felt so joyful in the whole of his life.

But he still had one more thing to do. He took the cages, one after another, and broke them into little pieces. The wood need not be wasted, though. It would heat his stove in the winter.

"Now there are a couple of dozen fewer animal prisons in the world," he said cheerfully, and mopped his brow.

The sun was high above the horizon when Anton set off for home. Suddenly—what was that?—one small brown bird had not gone with the others; it was fluttering over his head. "Well, little one," said Anton, "don't you want to fly away too?" But the bird seemed to have other ideas. As the old man left for home it followed him, flying from branch to branch, all the way back.

The little bird was a nightingale, and it chose to stay with Anton, flying in and out of his house as it wished. Now and then the old man felt sad because he could no longer go to sea where he had learned to love freedom. But the nightingale understood, and would sing to him so beautifully that his heart grew light again. Listening to the singing, Anton would think again of the many birds he had freed from their cages, and would once again feel happy and contented. He could never lose the freedom he had given to the birds.

The fisherman and the nightingale lived together for many years, the happiest of friends. For all I know, they may be living there still.